THE FLOWER

by JOHN LIGHT   illustrated by LISA EVANS

Brigg lived in a small room in a big city.

Every day, he walked through the city to work.

Brigg worked in the library,
where dangerous books were stored.

One day, on a high shelf in a dim cellar,
he found some books marked: 'Do not read'.

So Brigg smuggled one out of the library,
and took it home.

He read it in secret.

It showed pictures of the most beautiful
shapes and colours, and called them flowers.

Brigg felt sad
that there were no
flowers in the city.

He supposed
that was why the book
had been hidden away.

He wandered down many
streets, searching for
some sign of a flower.

In an old part of the city, he came to a junk shop ...

...and there in the window was a dusty picture of a flower.

Brigg went into the shop and bought the picture.

When he got home,
he looked at the back of it.
It said: 'Seeds'. Brigg felt very
excited about what they might be.

He opened the packet and tipped out seven
brown wrinkled things. On the back of the picture,
it said 'Cover with earth. Water.'

Brigg collected dust from all over the city …
…until he had enough to fill a mug.

He buried the seeds in it and added water.

Nothing happened.
Brigg was very disappointed.

He thought the seeds must be dead.
He left the mug on his table.

Then, when he woke up one morning,
he saw just one beautiful green shoot.

It grew and grew, and whenever
he was not at work or asleep, Brigg
sat and stared at the fresh green leaves.

At last the plant flowered.
Brigg was overjoyed.

But one morning, while Brigg was at work,
the room cleaning system came on
and the plant was sucked away.

When Brigg got home, he cried.

At last, he dried his eyes. He set off to search for another picture of flowers. After many weeks, he came to the edge of the city where the dust heaps were.

There, at the top of one of the huge dusty slopes,
Brigg found his dead flower.
At first, he felt sad. But when he looked closer,
he saw that there were new green shoots
and flowers all around. Brigg sat and looked
at them, until it was much too dark to see.

And he wondered how long it would take to fill a city with flowers.